Sailing the high seas . . .

"I think," said Lois deeply and thoughtfully, in her psychic mood, "I think what your parents should do next with their money is go on a long vacation."

She stopped her swing by dragging her feet on the ground. She stared into space. "I think I see water," she said. "I think I see a big, big boat. I think . . ."

Here her voice trailed off, because just then Mr. Green came around the side of the house. He was waving something. As he got closer, Daisy could see it was little folders. On the folders were pictures. And the pictures were of—was it possible?—ships!

"Guess what?" he asked. "The Bon Voyage cruise-ship company has asked us to make a TV commercial about how lottery winners choose their company for the vacation of a lifetime! They will pay all our expenses. It looks like we are off for a vacation on the high seas!"

LOTTERY LUCK

SHIP AHOY!

#5

Judy Delton

Illustrated by S. D. Schindler

Hyperion Paperbacks for Children
New York

First Hyperion Paperback edition 1995

Text © 1995 by Judy Delton.
Illustrations © 1995 by S. D. Schindler.

Printed in the United States of America.

1 3 5 7 9 10 8 6 4 2

The text for this book is set in 14-point Joanna
Designed by Yolanda Monteza.

Library of Congress Cataloging-in-Publication Data
Delton, Judy.
Ship ahoy! / Judy Delton ; illustrated by S.D. Schindler. — 1st ed.
p.   cm. — (Lottery luck ; #5)
Summary: As a result of winning the lottery the Green family goes on a two-week pleasure cruise, during which Aunt Ivy causes much commotion and excitement.
ISBN 0-7868-1022-X
[1. Ocean liners—Fiction.   2. Aunts—Fiction.   3. Lotteries—Fiction.   4. Family life—Fiction.]   I. Schindler, S. D., ill.
II. Title.   III. Series: Delton, Judy.   Lottery luck ; #5.
PZ7.D388Sh   1995
[Fic]—dc20   95-3285

For dear friends Kathy, Bev, Joan P.
On this we always will agree:
In Twine Ball Inn or in a Ford
The Word is mightier than the sword.

—J. D.

LOTTERY LUCK

SHIP AHOY!

#5

2

9

"The first thing I think we should do," said Lois to her best friend, Daisy, "is go shopping in the Mall of America."

Daisy had just moved to St. Paul from Liberty, Minnesota. Her family had won ten million dollars in the lottery, and that money had caused a lot of changes in their lives (and a lot of trouble). They were on the *Oriole Humphrey Show* in New York, solved a hotel mystery, had lots of strangers come and move in with them, and this was the biggest change. Leaving Liberty. Daisy's now-extended family had outgrown their condo. Her dad's three-piece bronze garden sculptures had filled their tiny living room and dining room until the family couldn't eat without a sculpture looking over their shoulders.

Then he was offered a wonderful opportunity at a big garden store in the city, and they had had to move. Now they had lots of room on the hobby farm they'd purchased.

And the good news was that Lois's family had *also* moved—to Minneapolis, the twin city of St. Paul—and the friends were back together again.

"I don't like malls," Daisy replied. "I like the little stores in Liberty, on Main Street."

Lois waved her words away. "They don't have good clothes," she said. "Their stuff is all out-of-date. And the mall has a real roller coaster and theater for when you're through shopping. I can't wait."

Daisy felt cross. She had thought the "I can't wait" things Lois would want to do together again would be long bike rides and trips to the library to get books by their favorite authors. (For all she knew, the library here was in a mall.)

"Like, I need curtains for my room, and a matching bedspread. The stuff from Liberty doesn't fit in our new place," Lois went on.

They were in Lois's new house. Daisy and her brother, Delphie, were helping Lois unpack. Lois's mother brought them a bowl filled with pretzels that had mustard built right in, as well as some cans of cream soda.

"There are so many new foods in Minneapolis!"

Lois's mother exclaimed. "Byerly's aisles are filled with fresh fish and artichokes and anchovies and all types of foreign foods that we can't wait to try!"

It was no wonder that Lois knew so many things, thought Daisy. Having parents who ate artichokes and anchovies was bound to rub off on her. It wasn't far from anchovies to ESP and psychic personalities or even real estate. Lois knew a lot. She knew how to stage houses when you sold them and how to use ESP to get your parents to actually think about buying a new house.

Lois unpacked a big carton of clothes and hung them in her new closet. It didn't look to Daisy like Lois needed to go to the mall. At least not to buy clothes.

"I love it here already," Lois chattered away. "My new school is only a block from here. It's huge."

"We have to ride the bus," said Delphie. He unpacked Lois's books and, after Lois dusted them, put them on the white bookshelves.

"There!" said Daisy, putting Lois's pencils and pens into her desk drawer. "This box is empty."

"Are there any more of these?" asked Delphie, cramming a handful of pretzels into his mouth.

"Artie doesn't have snacks around the house,"

said Daisy, trying to explain why Delphie was so unmannerly. Artie Fox was a long-lost cousin of the Greens' who had looked them up and moved in after he had seen them on the *Oriole Humphrey Show*. He was a good cook and gardener, but he was a vegetarian, and the family missed snacks and pork chops.

"Artie's like your aunt Ivy," said Lois. "Does she still drink those Rabbit Rousers?"

"They don't have them here," said Daisy. "But she gets Beta Bouncers, and they are just as bad."

"Carrot juice, yuck," said Delphie. "I like soda pop."

Lois went and filled the pretzel dish and also brought in some little crackers that had cheese built into the middle.

Lois's dad came and took the empty cartons away and said, "What help you two have been. We'll be settled in no time."

When he had left, Lois looked at her watch and said, "I think we need a break. It's almost time for your dad to come and get you. Let's go out in the yard and swing till he comes."

The people who lived there before Lois had left three swings hanging from a very tall oak tree. They went much, much higher than little swings on a swing set. These were grown-up swings for adults. It would figure that Lois's new house would have special things, thought Daisy. Special things happened to psychic people.

The swings swished up into the high tree branches and then swooped down like big birds.

"Your house is really nice," said Daisy.

"Not as nice as yours," said Lois. "You've got a guest house and barns, and you can even keep ponies."

Daisy didn't want to argue about whose house was best.

"And it's about time your parents got that new, bigger place," Lois went on. "I thought they would never move from that tiny condo. I mean that's why we asked Aunt Ivy to buy them the lottery ticket in the first place. So you could get out of there."

"If it wasn't for Artie and Gladys and Roxanne and Olivia, we'd still be in the cozy condo in Liberty," said Daisy. "But when they came and moved in, it really was crowded."

"Well, it's not crowded now," said Lois. "There's room for even more relatives to move in."

Daisy frowned. She didn't want any more relatives to come.

"What do you think your parents will do next with their lottery money?" asked Lois.

"What do you mean?" asked Daisy. She hated change and she didn't like the word *next*. Things were just fine now. As Aunt Ivy said, "Let sleeping dogs lie." She saw that on *Wheel of Fortune*.

Lois sighed. "You've still got lots of money from the lottery in the bank. I mean, it keeps earning more and more interest. And now your dad is selling a lot of his garden creatures, so you've got even *more* money."

"It's for college," said Daisy. "They are saving it for college."

"Pooh," said Lois, dismissing college without a thought. "That's a long way off. Besides, there's plenty for that, too. I mean your house didn't cost ten million dollars. And you can get a scholarship; you're real smart."

That was the thing about Lois. She had an answer for everything. And she was usually right.

"What's 'scholarship'?" asked Delphie. "Is it like a battleship? We don't need a boat to go to college. We can walk or take a plane."

"It's not a boat," said Lois. "It's money they pay you to go to college."

"They can't pay me to go to college," said Delphie. "I'm sick of school."

"I think," said Lois deeply and thoughtfully, in her psychic mood, "I think what your parents should do next with their money is go on a long vacation."

She stopped her swing by dragging her feet on the ground. She stared into space. "I think I see water," she said. "I think I see a big, big boat. I think . . ."

Here her voice trailed off, because just then Mr. Green came around the side of the house. He was waving something. As he got closer, Daisy could see it was little folders. On the folders were pictures. And the pictures were of—was it possible?—ships!

"Guess what?" he asked. "The Bon Voyage cruise-ship company has asked us to make a TV commercial about how lottery winners choose their company for the vacation of a lifetime! They will pay all our expenses. It looks like we are off for a vacation on the high seas!"

CHAPTER 2

Daisy groaned. Lois's magic had struck again. And this time it meant more change, as usual. If there was one thing Daisy did not need or want, it was new excitement. The lottery and New York *and* moving were enough to last a lifetime.

But here was Lois, and even her own sweet father, already hustling all of them onto an ocean liner, to sail to someplace they had never heard of, on a vacation they didn't need.

"What's 'bon voyage'?" Delphie was shouting.

"'Bon voyage' means 'good-bye and have a good trip,'" said Lois. "I knew I saw water! And the boat I saw said 'Bon Voyage' on the side of it! When do you sail, Mr. Green?"

"We sail a week from Saturday, from Miami, Florida, if we can all get ready by then," said Daisy's father. "Aunt Ivy will have to take time off from her new job, and we have to see how your parents feel, Lois, about sending you on a Caribbean cruise!"

"Me?" said Lois, pointing to herself. "I'm coming, too?"

"Of course," said Mr. Green. "You are the one responsible for all of this excitement!"

Daisy was very glad to hear her best friend was coming, too, but she didn't know why Lois was surprised. Being psychic, she must have known she would be included. Maybe she was just being polite, thought Daisy.

"Are we going on the *Love Boat?*" demanded Delphie. "Can Larkspur come? And Artie and Olivia and Sophy?"

"No dogs on board," laughed his dad. "Or cats. And I'm afraid it just includes our family and Lois. It's not the *Love Boat*, but it will be a ship just like that. There's a lot to talk about. Maybe Lois could come and spend the night with you, Daisy, while we plan the trip."

Lois ran to ask her mom if she could go to the Greens', and Mr. Green talked to Lois's dad about letting Lois take the trip. "We'll be back before school starts," said Mr. Green.

"What a seasoned traveler my daughter is becoming!" laughed Lois's dad. "Well, travel is educational. And it's an experience of a lifetime."

As far as Daisy could see, Lois didn't need any more education. Or experience. She already had done far more, and knew far more, than anyone else Daisy had ever met.

"Will I be seasoned, too?" cried Delphie. Then he frowned. "What is 'seasoned'?" he asked.

Everyone laughed. Adults thought Delphie said cute things. Daisy was disgusted. Delphie knew he was cute, she thought, and liked the attention.

"We're going to season you with salt and pepper and put you on the grill," said his sister meanly.

Delphie gave out a howl and looked ready to cry.

"'Seasoned' means an experienced traveler," said his dad, frowning at Daisy. "Not a spicy piece of meat."

Lois's parents were very excited about the cruise news and read the brochures Mr. Green had brought.

"Wow!" said Lois. "The ship is eight hundred feet long!"

"It weighs over sixty thousand tons!" said her dad.

"It says about fifteen hundred people go on

every cruise," said her mother. "That's a lot of people on one boat. There are seven hundred cabins!"

"Do we get a bed to sleep in?" asked Delphie.

Daisy wanted to ask the same question. She had no idea what a big ship was like.

"We will each have a bed," laughed Mr. Green. "We will have a big suite of rooms, I understand, like in the hotel in New York."

Now Daisy was baffled. How could a boat have room enough for fifteen hundred people?

"There are swimming pools on those ships," said Lois. "I've seen pictures of them."

"Ours even has a small golf course on the top deck," said Mr. Green.

Daisy and Delphie were speechless. But Lois and the others were chatting like it was a normal thing for a ship to have these things. Swimming pools and golf courses all floating along right on top of the water.

"Can we fish from the boat?" asked Delphie.

"That's probably the only thing we can't do," laughed his dad. "The thing one usually does from a boat is the one thing no one does on a cruise ship. At least I don't think so."

Lois ran and got her pajamas and put them in her overnight bag. Mr. Green left some brochures and also the name of the ship and its cruising dates and phone numbers with Lois's parents. Then he herded the three children into the car and started for the Greens' house.

"See you tomorrow," called Lois, waving to her parents.

Mr. Green drove over a bridge that separated Minneapolis from St. Paul. Underneath the bridge was the Mississippi River.

"This great river starts in our state of Minnesota," said Mr. Green. "Up north at Itasca Park the river is just a little puddle of water you can step over."

Daisy wished they could take the riverboat that she could see below them. It was big and white and, best of all, it was close to home. If it was good enough for Tom Sawyer, it was good enough for her.

But all the way to Winner's Roost, Lois read the brochures out loud and pointed to the pictures.

"We have to go all the way to Florida to board the boat," she said. Then she read, "'A glass elevator takes you soaring up high above the sea. There on the top deck you can play golf, lounge in a deck chair, eat in our Ocean Breeze dining room, or order deck service.'"

Delphie whistled his long, low whistle. "An elevator on a *boat!*" he exclaimed.

Lois continued, " 'Then you may want to get in shipshape by working out in our state-of-the-art gymnasium. You may also enjoy having an herbal-therapy massage or just relaxing in our Norwegian sauna.' "

Here Lois showed a picture of six people smiling, all having a massage. Two of the people had gray hair, two were little children, and two must have been the children's parents. They all had very, very white teeth.

"Fun for the entire family," it said under the picture.

The same family was on the next page helping themselves to appetizers from a long table loaded with sizzling steaks and fried chicken, golden shrimp and beef roasts, pasta, and even giant strawberries dipped in chocolate. There were beautiful flowers on the table, too, and drinks with umbrellas in them.

"Yum," said Lois. "I can't wait to go on this ship!"

Mr. Green turned down their own little lane and drove up in front of the door of their new house. Aunt Ivy—with a sailor hat on her head instead of her meter-maid cap—was out in front waving at them.

"Ship ahoy!" she called, saluting.

Daisy was pretty sure Aunt Ivy had heard the news.

CHAPTER 3

Aunt Ivy was living with the Greens until she got her own apartment in St. Paul. She had been the meter maid in Liberty, and now she had gotten a job as a meter maid in St. Paul. She was also going to night school to become a private eye.

Artie came out of the front door to meet them, too. And behind him was Gladys Gunder, who had just come home from work.

Gladys had seen the Greens on TV when they won the lottery, and she had come to their door with her cat, Sophy. She had gone to high school with Mr. Green years ago.

The last ones to move in were Roxanne and her baby, Olivia. Roxanne was from England.

"Fan!" said Olivia when she saw Daisy. Fan was Olivia's only word so far. She said it when she saw the fans in the ceiling of the house or when she saw someone she liked. Sometimes she said it if she was very excited or if she ate some food she liked. Sometimes she just said it for no reason at all.

Daisy's mother rushed out of the house as well.

"Did you hear the news?" she said.

Daisy nodded. Lois and Delphie shouted, "Yeah!"

Everyone trooped into the dining room for Artie's dinner. They all talked at once.

"I wish we could take everyone," said Mrs. Green, passing Artie's stir-fry around the table. "But we need Artie here to look after the house, tend our new garden, feed Larkspur, and take orders for Dad."

Larkspur heard his name, came out from under the table, and barked.

"I'm glad to do all that," said Artie. "I get seasick just riding in a car," he laughed.

"And I can't get away from my new job," said Gladys. "It's too soon for a paid vacation."

"Mine, too," said Roxanne. "And Olivia is too young to travel."

"They are letting me have the time off," said Aunt Ivy, stabbing a bean sprout with her fork, "but I'm sure they hate to see me go. They realize what a valuable worker I am, with all my experience on the Liberty force."

It sounded like Aunt Ivy was on the police force, thought Daisy. The meter-maid division was a part of the police department, it was true, but a meter maid was definitely not a policeman. No matter how much Aunt Ivy would like to think so.

"And of course I'll have to miss my night-school classes," she went on. "Perhaps I can do some work on the ship, some on-the-spot investigating."

Oh no, thought Daisy. Aunt Ivy would be suspecting everyone on board of a crime, like she had in New York! And if there was a real crime, she would end up befriending the criminal! Just like she had in New York.

"Well, the Bon Voyage folks want us aboard the *Island Maiden* next Saturday. That should bring us back in plenty of time for the start of school."

"Why, just look at this!" said Roxanne as Artie brought in dessert. She held up a brochure. "There's a full-size theater on board the *Island Maiden*. And a whole wing for the children's activities, including full-time supernannies!"

"I don't need a nanny!" cried Delphie.

"The nannies plan games, treasure hunts, shuffleboard tournaments, and all kinds of activities. And they make you great snacks," said Mr. Green.

Delphie's mood changed. "Really?" he said. "Treasure hunts?"

His dad nodded.

"'It is our goal to serve you,'" read Gladys. "'Your wish is our command. Our staff is on board to make your cruise vacation the most memorable of your life. That is our wish and our commitment.'"

Mrs. Green looked dreamy, as if she was already relaxing to the ripple of the waves and the music of the seas.

"'What will you do first every morning?'" read Gladys. "'Will you have breakfast in bed with a rose on your tray? An early walk on the deck watching the sunrise over the sea? An aerobics class in the gym? A game of water polo?

"'Or maybe you want all of these. It's up to you.'"

Now Mrs. Green's eyes were closed. She had a smile on her face. Maybe her mother did need a vacation, thought Daisy. The move had been hard work, and the new garden was a big job. If her sweet mother would enjoy the cruise, the least Daisy could do was to act like she wanted to go.

"Now the thing we must guard against is sea-sickness," said Aunt Ivy. "I myself have a stomach of steel. But I have homemade herbal remedies that I'll bring along for the children. And it seems to me, Iris, that you used to get a little upset on the Ferris wheel as a child. Fortunately, I have just the thing. And as soon as we are aboard, I will lead you in exercises doing deep breathing."

After the girls helped Artie and Roxanne clear the table and load the dishwasher, they went to Daisy's room.

"What if we get seasick?" said Daisy.

"Pooh, I don't get seasick. Do you get sick on rides at the fair?" Lois demanded.

Daisy shook her head. "I don't think so," she said.

"Then you won't get sick at sea," said Lois. "Anyway we can get that stuff for motion sickness from the drugstore."

"Aunt Ivy says that's no good," said Daisy.

But Lois was busy looking through Daisy's closet to see what was suitable for the cruise.

"We *have* to go to the Mall of America," she said. "We need new stuff for the trip. You should see how people dress up on ships. The women wear long dresses and the men wear tuxes and there are big dances every night."

"I can't dance," said Daisy. "And I know Delphie can't."

"You don't have to dance," said Lois. "But we want to look good. We can't wear stuff we wore in Liberty on a cruise."

When the girls got into bed, they couldn't sleep. There was too much to think about. The pictures of the Island Maiden in the brochures kept flashing in Daisy's mind. She remembered the new friends she'd just made in St. Paul. She would have to send them postcards. She would hate to have them forget her so soon. And she wanted Lois to meet them. So far, there had been no time.

"We can go to the mall together. Your mom, my mom, and your aunt Ivy," said Lois. "We have to be sure Aunt Ivy doesn't wear that meter-maid uniform on the trip again."

Lois had mall on the brain. Daisy didn't care if she never even saw the biggest mall in America.

"Aunt Ivy has other clothes," laughed Daisy. "She just thinks her uniform makes her look official. She thinks it looks like a police uniform."

If Lois was obsessed with malls, Aunt Ivy was

obsessed with detective work. Daisy wondered what she herself was obsessed with. Then she remembered: worry. That's what she did most of the time. Her mother said it was a waste of time, and so did Lois, but she couldn't stop. Now she secretly worried that her new friends would forget her, that the Island Maiden would sink, that Delphie would fall overboard, and that everyone would know how to act on the boat except her.

"Do you know what?" said Lois. "The cruise-ship company is paying for this whole trip because of the commercial."

"I know," said Daisy. "They will show our pictures and say that lottery winners choose Bon Voyage for cruises. They'll show us on TV having a lot of fun. Except we didn't actually choose them. They chose us." Daisy frowned. She wondered if that was a lie.

"You know what that means?" said Lois. "It means your folks don't have to take any of their lottery money out of the bank to pay for the trip. It means it's all there for you to use on something else."

"It's for college," Daisy reported. She liked to tell herself that so that the big bankroll would not bring on even more changes.

Finally, both she and Lois drifted off to sleep. Daisy dreamed that everyone missed the boat but her. As it sailed away, she saw her loved ones waving from the dock. Everyone but her was on board with their family, and everyone was wearing white sailor outfits. Daisy was wearing her pajamas. The ship's captain said she had to get off at the first island they came to, and when she woke up in the morning, she thought the captain was still chasing her down the gangplank.

If this was a psychic prediction like Lois's, it looked like this trip was off to a bad start.

CHAPTER 4

The following week was filled with planning and shopping and packing. Daisy, Lois, and Delphie went to the Mall of America with Aunt Ivy. The girls worried that Delphie would get lost in such a large place. But he didn't. It was Aunt Ivy who got lost. One minute she was at their side, and the next minute she was gone.

When they finally found her, she said crossly, "You must learn to not wander off. You could have been lost for good!"

After everyone got a new bathing suit and some matching shorts-and-tops outfits, and Delphie bought a few small water toys, they all had lunch in Snoopyland. They sat on stools shaped like animals and ordered hamburgers named Lucyburgers and Brownburgers. Aunt Ivy fussed because they did not have vegetarian lunches and Rabbit Rouser carrot juice.

"This is not a pasta palace," said the manager. "We have fun food here."

"And you'll be sorry for that someday when all of your teeth fall out," said Aunt Ivy, shaking a finger at him.

"I wish you and I could shop alone," whispered Lois in Daisy's ear. "This place is full of great places your aunt won't go."

"When we get back from the cruise, I'll ask my mom to drop us off for the day," said Daisy. "All alone. Aunt Ivy is too much responsibility."

When they got home, they showed everyone their purchases, and Delphie asked if they could leave Aunt Ivy home next time they went to the mall.

The week flew by, and suitcases got packed. Mr. Green came home with sailor hats for everyone. Delphie's was a captain's cap.

On Friday, Mrs. Green put lists on the refrigerator for Artie, Gladys, and Roxanne. The lists said which days to water the indoor plants, what to feed Larkspur, and the dates and times of arrival and departure of the ship and planes. They had telephone numbers for emergencies and directions on how to contact the ship in case the house burned down. Daisy privately thought it would be better not to know things like this, since they could not get back from the middle of an ocean to do anything about it.

Finally, Saturday came, and everyone was out in front of the house to say "Bon voyage." Lois's parents had brought Lois over in the morning, so they were there to see them off, too.

Just as they were about to leave, Bunny, Mrs. Green's new neighborhood friend, came running down the lane, pulling her nephew Warren, who had an overbite and did not talk. Warren did not look like he wanted to be there. Bunny had an armful of flowers and a big cake with the words Have a Good Trip in red frosting.

Then Chelsea's dad (he owned the shop that sold Mr. Green's garden animals) drove up with Chelsea to say good-bye.

"Oh, I'm so glad to meet Lois," she said, pumping her hand. "That's a great outfit! My aunt went on a cruise, and she met a guy who worked for the government, I think he was a senator or something and . . ."

Daisy was glad that her new friend had not forgotten her, but the friend she really wished was there was someone Delphie had brought home. Mavis was a sister of Miles's, Delphie's friend. Perhaps she forgot that Daisy was leaving on a cruise. Or maybe she was busy with all her other friends and forgot all about her.

But all of a sudden, as they drove down their driveway on the way to the Twin Cities International Airport, Mavis came along on her bike. She was carrying a package that was wrapped like a gift. Daisy opened the car window, and Mavis handed it to her.

"Have a good trip," she shyly said to Daisy. "I'll miss you."

"See you as soon as I get back," said Daisy, reaching out the window and giving Mavis a hug. Daisy opened the package as they drove along. It was a little travel alarm clock.

"I hope we aren't late," said Aunt Ivy, looking at her watch.

"There's always time for our good-byes," said Mr. Green.

Aunt Ivy was annoying Daisy already, and they had not even left. After all, Daisy was lucky to have such good friends. At least Aunt Ivy was not wearing her meter-maid uniform. She was wearing just the little pin of merit she'd received from the Liberty police for apprehending a man who was putting fake quarters into the parking meters.

They got to the airport safely, and in plenty of time. Mr. Green had everyone's tickets, and they went to gate twenty-three and boarded the plane. This was old hat to the family now since their trip to New York when Aunt Ivy had practiced being a detective on the plane and had caused a small emergency.

This time they sat down and fastened their seat belts and read the emergency information on the charts provided. They kept their seats in an upright position and ordered soda pop, and Delphie did not shout out things like "Look at the little oven!" as he had done before.

In fact, they were off the ground and in the air and sipping their sodas before any crisis at all occurred.

CHAPTER 5

Suddenly, however, there was a piercing scream, one long shriek and then four short ones. Daisy did not have to turn around to know who it was. The voice was familiar.

"Help!" shouted the voice.

"Are we in trouble?" shouted the passengers across the aisle from Daisy.

Daisy shook her head. "It's just my aunt Ivy," she said to comfort them.

Now people were out of their seats and passing rumors that there was engine trouble.

The flight attendant shepherded everyone to their seat. "There is no engine trouble," she said firmly. "We are perfectly safe. The trouble is here on board." She glared at Aunt Ivy.

"Stop this plane!" shouted Aunt Ivy. "My handbag is missing! I have to go back and find it!"

Mr. Green hurried to Aunt Ivy's seat and tried to calm her.

"Did you have it when we boarded?" he asked.

Aunt Ivy shook her head. "I left it home. It is on the kitchen table." Here Aunt Ivy wailed some more, thinking of her purse so far away. "I had my cruise ticket in it, and my traveler's checks and my birth certificate and honorary awards and my passport and my library card! I'm no good without my official documents!"

"Do we need a passport to take a cruise?" asked Lois, frowning.

"I don't think so," said Daisy.

Now Aunt Ivy was quietly weeping into Mr. Green's big white handkerchief.

"You won't need your library card, Ivy," said her sister, trying to comfort her. But Ivy was not to be comforted.

"Perhaps you left it in the car," said Mr. Green. "Or at the airport when we checked in."

"It's at home," Aunt Ivy sobbed. "I have to get off this plane!" She got out of her seat and began to walk toward the door.

"You can't just open the door in the middle of the sky and get out like you're on a bus," said

Delphie in disgust. "There's no station in the sky."
Aunt Ivy irritated him. She was so unreasonable.

"Well," said Lois, looking at her watch, "it took your aunt Ivy exactly twenty minutes to create a crisis this trip. She is right on schedule."

All of the flight attendants were gathered around Aunt Ivy now, and even one of the co-pilots had come out of the cockpit to see what was going on.

"We can't turn a plane around, ma'am," he said. "But when you land in Miami, you can call home and trace it. And we'll check with the desk at the airport."

"If it is at home, we can always have Gladys send it express delivery to you in Miami," said Mr. Green.

Daisy was sure they could not express something in a few hours. Their cruise ship left this very afternoon.

"Well, we've searched the plane," said a flight attendant, "The purse does not seem to be on board. It's not in the overhead bins or under the seats or in the wardrobe closets."

"I know that," said Aunt Ivy. "It's home on the table."

"Well, there's nothing we can do about it

now," said Mrs. Green. "We'll just have to wait till we get to Miami and work something out."

It was hard to enjoy the flight now, with Aunt Ivy sobbing quietly behind them, thought Daisy.

But Lois and Delphie didn't have any trouble. They had maps out showing the ship's route and were studying the itinerary.

"Here's where we land first," said Lois, pointing to an island that was just a little dot on the map. "We get off the boat for a couple of hours. It says here they have fishing boats for rent, Delph; you might be able to fish, after all."

"Yea!" shouted Delphie. Then he quickly changed his smile to a sad look when he saw how miserable his aunt was.

But before long he, Daisy, and Lois were smiling again, looking at the brochures.

"This is what I'm having from the buffet," said Lois, giving the brochure a stab with her finger. With her pencil she checked off some of the colorful foods on the buffet table. "Tacos, shrimp, and guacamole for appetizers. Then crabmeat salad—I love that stuff! Also, this rib roast with the little paper doilies on it, and potatoes au gratin, peas, and for dessert, this specialty of the ship, mimosa mousse! Doesn't that sound good? My mouth is watering!"

"I'm going to get this hamburger and fries," said Delphie. "I'm not eating any old moose."

As they talked about the shipboard meals, the flight attendant brought them little wet towels and a tray with their lunch on it.

By the time they all had finished eating, the captain announced they were about to land in Miami.

"The temperature is eighty-five degrees, sunny skies, and there are no clouds in sight. Please leave your seats in an upright position, fasten your seat belts, and do not disembark until the plane is stopped at the terminal. Have a good trip, and thank you for flying our airline today."

People were busy combing their hair and collecting their carry-on luggage. Mr. Green helped the family get the suitcases from under their seats. Aunt Ivy put hers on the seat next to her and opened it to get some tissues to wipe her teary eyes.

As she did, her face turned beet red. Daisy wondered if the anxiety was too much for her.

"My goodness," said Aunt Ivy in surprise and dismay, "look what I found in my suitcase!"

She reached into the case and held up the missing handbag—the handbag that was supposed to be home on the table—for everyone to see.

CHAPTER 6

Everyone was angry with Aunt Ivy but tried not to show it.

"I could strangle your aunt!" said Lois. "After all that fuss!"

"Well, good for you, Ivy!" said her sister. "I'm so glad the problem is solved."

"Just hold on to that purse now," warned Mr. Green. "Let's all get onto that ship safely."

A taxicab took the family to the dock, where lots of people were hugging their loved ones and saying good-bye. There were streamers and flags flying from the ship, and a band on one of the decks was playing "Anchors Aweigh."

"Wow!" shouted Delphie. "That is one huge ship!"

Daisy could not believe how big the boat looked. It was bigger than a hotel. It was bigger than a city block! It was bigger than their entire

hobby farm! And it was very, very white. It looked so clean and white that it dazzled in the sun. Someone must have scrubbed it that very morning, although Daisy could not imagine how anyone could reach that high. It would have had to be a giant.

Everyone was having a good time. Men dressed in naval uniforms with stripes on their sleeves and sailor hats on their heads were shaking passengers' hands and welcoming them aboard. The noise and music was deafening. It sounded like there was a huge celebration, like the pictures Daisy had seen on TV of New Year's Eve in Times Square.

"That's the A Deck," said Lois, pointing. "And that's the Promenade Deck right above it."

"Where are the bedrooms?" asked Delphie.

"The cabins are on the Bridge Deck and the Commodore Deck," Lois answered. "Way in front are the fancy suites, where the rich people stay."

"That's us," said Delphie.

Their dad looked surprised. Then he said, "I guess it is! We are staying in the deluxe suite with a private veranda. Our suite number is 7000, on the Bridge Deck."

As the Greens came aboard, two officers who

looked as clean and scrubbed as the boat greeted them. They had tanned skin, as if they were in the sun a long time. One of them, named Ralph, pointed to Aunt Ivy and said, "I've heard all about you! I hear you tried to turn the plane around, on the flight to Miami!"

"It was an emergency," said Aunt Ivy, turning red.

Ralph laughed. "Do you know what they're calling you around here?" he laughed. "Poison Ivy! Only in fun, of course!"

Aunt Ivy didn't look like it was fun.

"I was called that as a child," she said. "And it scarred my life."

So Aunt Ivy's behavior was not new, thought Daisy! She had been this way all her life! And the flight crew and the ship's crew knew it already!

Daisy felt sorry for her aunt. It could not be fun to be the butt of a joke all the time. Aunt Ivy was right—things like that did leave a scar. Poison ivy was something (or someone!) no one wanted to be near.

Ralph went on to greet another passenger, and the other officer turned to the Greens and said, "Welcome to the *Island Maiden*. We hope you enjoy cruising with us."

"I'm sure we will," said Mr. Green.

Then a woman who was also in a white uniform handed Aunt Ivy and Mrs. Green each a big bouquet of flowers and said, "We hope your trip with us will be a memorable one."

With Aunt Ivy aboard, Daisy was pretty sure it would be. Even if Aunt Ivy did not get into any more trouble at all, it would be memorable. This boat was something people from Liberty, Minnesota, did not see often.

The woman sailor, who said to call her Sally, acted as if the Greens were her only passengers. She gave them a map of the ship, explained what activities were planned for the day, invited them to have a snack by the pool, and then led them onto the glass elevator and down the hall to suite 7000. She unlocked the door, and they entered a room that was flooded with sunlight. Outside the sliding glass doors was a private deck and a view of what looked like the entire ocean. The waves lapped against the ship, and Daisy noticed that when she walked, it was easy to lose her balance.

"Well, you'll have to excuse me," said Aunt Ivy, "I have to do my breathing exercises before I can sightsee."

She went into the bedroom that was hers, and

everyone could hear her breathing deeply.

"This boat tips," said Delphie, grabbing onto a chair.

"It's brewing up something out there," said Sally cheerfully.

When Daisy looked at the sea, it was as if the boat was not straight. One end was higher than the other. The next time she looked, the other end was up. If the boat was crooked when it was in the harbor, what would it be on the open sea? She had read that harbors are protected. Whatever was "brewing up" out there, was probably not going to go away when they set sail. Daisy could hear the wind whistling around the windows—or portholes, as they were called on a ship.

"It will take a while," said Mr. Green. "But we will get our sea legs eventually."

"Look at the fireplace!" Delphie pointed. "A fireplace on a boat!"

"That will take the chill off if you feel cold in the early morning," said Sally. She was unpacking the large suitcases that had already arrived.

On the table in front of the fireplace was a bottle of champagne resting in an ice bucket, little round snacks with small fish on them, and another bouquet of flowers.

"If you are hungry in the middle of the night," said Sally, "you can raid this little refrigerator." She swung open the door of what looked like a piece of furniture in someone's living room, but inside a light came on, and it was jam-packed with food.

"Of course you can always call room service, day or night, and we'll bring you what you are hungry for. That's what we're here for, to make your trip a memorable one."

Outside, whistles began to blow. Long, low, deep whistles.

"That's the first warning to visitors to leave the ship," said Sally.

Sure enough, when Mr. Green opened the door, they all heard "All ashore that's going ashore," from staff members out in the hall and on the decks.

The low, sad whistle continued to blow. Stepping out on the veranda, the girls saw people below hurrying off the boat, and others giving friends a last-minute hug.

"Now," said Sally, "you are wanted on the B Deck, to film the lottery winners leaving on their trip of a lifetime."

Aunt Ivy was summoned from her exercises,

and Sally helped everyone wash up and comb their hair and straighten their shirts.

But out on the deck, it was so windy that their hair was soon frowsy again. Three cameramen videotaped the Greens coming out of their cabin, leaning over the deck waving, and later back in their room, in front of the fireplace, opening the champagne and toasting to a fine trip.

"We'll be filming by the pool and at the buffet as the trip goes on," said Sally. "But now we'll leave you to meet other guests and enjoy the start of your vacation."

"We're moving!" shouting Delphie from the veranda. "Ship ahoy!"

He waved to the people on shore. The gangplank was gone, and the Island Maiden glided out of the harbor.

"This is like a ride at the fair!" said Delphie, stumbling along the deck from side to side.

"It isn't any worse than on an elevator in the IDS Building in St. Paul," said Daisy.

Lois nodded. "It's fun," she said. "Like riding the roller coaster or the Ferris wheel without paying."

The children walked up and down deck B and studied the map. They checked the pool and had a snack from the table beside it.

When they came back to their suite, there was a low moan coming from one of the bedrooms. Mrs. Green put her fingers to her lips.

"Sssh," she whispered. "It's Aunt Ivy."

"What's the matter with her?" asked Delphie.

Mrs. Green frowned. "I'm afraid she's seasick," she said. "The ship's doctor is in her room now."

CHAPTER 7

Aunt Ivy was in the sick bay the first day of the trip, and in her own bed the next. When she got up, her skin was a pale green color. She asked her family not to tell her how good the food was from the little refrigerator or from room service or from the buffet. In fact, she didn't want to hear about food at all.

"It's best not to eat much when a person is on a vacation," she said.

"By tomorrow you'll feel different," said Mr. Green. "You'll be begging for some of that catfish and grits for breakfast. They announced that the wind will be dying down late tonight."

Aunt Ivy had to admit she felt stronger the next day. "I believe it's my herbal remedy that's responsible," she said. "And I'm getting my sea legs at last."

As soon as Aunt Ivy had her sea legs, she set off with her notebook to explore the ship and watch and wait for any suspicious characters who might be looking for trouble.

"An ounce of prevention is worth a pound of cure," she said mysteriously. "I want to spot any criminals before they take advantage of any passenger."

"No crime is going to happen on this ship, Ivy," laughed Mr. Green.

But Aunt Ivy reminded him that no one thought the jewel thieves would be in their own hotel in New York, and they were.

"Thanks to our clever sleuthing and my expertise from detective class, we were able to apprehend them before they stole any more gems," said Aunt Ivy.

Daisy wondered about the word "our." It was she, Lois, and Delphie who had detected the robbers. At the time, Aunt Ivy was buying them dinner.

"I'm going to try out that golf course on the top deck this afternoon," said Mr. Green. "After some deck shuffleboard."

"I'm just going to stretch out in one of those big lounge chairs on the Commodore Deck and drink mimosas and read the new mystery I got in the ship's library," said Mrs. Green.

Just then there was a knock on the cabin door.

"Sally said the nanny would be coming by," she said.

"I don't want any old nanny!" said Delphie.

But when the nanny came in, he changed his mind. The nanny wasn't old, and he wasn't a woman.

"You must be the Greens," he said. "And here are Daisy and Delphie, and this must be Lois, the friend whose idea it was to buy that lottery ticket! Well my name is Otis, and wait till I show you what we've got going on in the Hot Spot."

Otis didn't look much older than Daisy and Lois, and he had a lot of pep.

Rubbing his hands together, he said, "First of all, we're organizing a treasure hunt. The one who finds the hidden medallion on board wins a great prize. We're also planning a Halloween masquerade party, with all kinds of costumes for you to choose from, and we need your help to make it work."

Delphie said, "I'm ready! Let's go!" And he bounded out the door ahead of Otis.

"And you girls," Otis went on. "Will you work with me, too?"

Daisy was cautious. "What's the Hot Spot?" she asked.

"That's the club where kids hang out, you know, to get away from the adults." Otis winked at the Greens. "We've got stuff going on there night and day. Any time you want action, that's where you come."

"I love action!" said Delphie.

"Good," laughed Otis, handing the Greens a map of how to find the Hot Spot, and a list of the activities that went on there.

"It's too early for Halloween," said Lois. "It's not for two months."

"We make our own holidays around here," said Otis. "Kids say Halloween is the best holiday of the year, so we celebrate it all year round, even in the summer! And sometimes, aboard the *Island Maiden*, we even have Christmas in July. You haven't lived till you've spent a New Year's Eve with us!"

"Can I come?" blurted out Aunt Ivy. "I love parties!"

"Sorry," said Otis. "No adults allowed in the Hot Spot."

Delphie breathed an audible sigh of relief. He didn't want his aunt at the Halloween party.

"You all go and have a good time," said Mrs. Green, getting out her swimsuit and sunglasses. "I'm off to relax in the sun. Ivy can come with me. We'll look at the bulletin board for some exciting adult activities. I'm sure there are parties for adults, too." She winked at Daisy.

"I love masquerades," said Lois to Daisy, on the way. "My aunt once won a prize when she went to one dressed as a stalk of celery."

When the children got to the Hot Spot, there were others already there. Other nannies were working with them. Delphie headed for a group of boys who were carving pumpkins with scary faces. Others were making life-size white ghosts and black witches for party decorations. Delphie chose a great big pumpkin, and Otis helped him carve it. He showed Delphie pictures of scary faces and said, "It's best to decide what kind of face you want before we carve. Think twice and cut once."

Sally was there, too, and showed the girls a huge walk-in closet, with costumes of all sorts hanging on racks. "You can look through these and mix and match things to create what you want to be," she

said. "But the important thing is, don't tell anyone what you choose. We want this to be a real surprise, where no one knows who you are. There will be a prize for the best costume."

When Sally left, Daisy said, "Boy, just look at all these outfits! There's Spiderman and Batman and Elvis and a whole row of ballerinas!"

The girls walked up one row and down another. First Daisy thought she'd like to be one of the seven dwarfs. But then she saw a whole aisle of animals: tigers, elephants, panthers, and alligators. "I could dress up like one of my dad's garden sculptures!" she said.

"Here is a whole row of food costumes," called Lois. "Even a tea-bag costume!"

"This is sure easier than making our own costumes like we did in Liberty," said Daisy.

"Sally said we can mix and match these," said Lois. "And make something original."

When the girls had finally decided on their costumes, Sally came in and hustled them off to fitting rooms, where a woman with pins took their costumes in here and let them out there. Then she gave them each a box to put their costume in so no one would see what they were going to wear. Before they left, Delphie chose his costume, too, and got it fitted.

"Now mum's the word," said Sally, putting her finger on her lips. "Don't even tell each other who you are going to be at the party."

"Or what we're going to be!" said Delphie.

"Especially Aunt Ivy," said Daisy.

"The big party will be at 7 P.M. on Friday," said Otis. "And before that, at 6 P.M. we go trick-or-treating at the cabins on the B Deck."

"Wow!" said Delphie. "This early Halloween is the best Halloween of all!"

"Tomorrow morning the treasure hunt begins, so be here at ten o'clock sharp," said Otis.

They started back to their cabin, but when they got off the glass elevator nothing looked familiar.

"This isn't our floor," said Lois. "It looks like the basement and it's very dark."

"You can't come down here," a man from out of the darkness said in a deep and scary voice. "This is off-limits to passengers."

He herded them back onto the elevator, and the door closed. The children were relieved when it opened again and they were on the Commodore Deck. Straight ahead was their sweet mother resting on a deck chair, reading her mystery and drinking her mimosa.

On the next chair, Aunt Ivy was taking notes.

"There's not much suspicious going on on the boat," she complained. "I probably won't have any mystery to work on this trip."

CHAPTER 8

The next morning Aunt Ivy bounced out of bed and into Daisy's room.

"Isn't today the day of the treasure hunt?" she asked.

Daisy stretched. She liked lying in bed on the boat and feeling the rock, rock, rocking of the waves and hearing the lap of the water below her bedroom.

"I guess so," said Daisy.

Aunt Ivy got out her notebook. "I've made a few notes of where it could be," she said. "Just to help you, of course," she added. "That's my specialty, you know, solving mysteries, finding clues."

Aunt Ivy was restless, thought Daisy, even on a boat with hundreds of planned activities. Daisy wished she could send her aunt off to do something else.

"I have listed the sections of the boat here,"

Aunt Ivy announced, "and then I have broken them down into possible hiding places for the medallion." She handed the list to Daisy. "If you need my help, I could try to work it into my schedule."

"This treasure hunt is for kids," said her niece kindly. "There are lots of adult activities listed on the bulletin board. There's karaoke in the lounge at ten and diving lessons by the pool at noon and even dance lessons on the B Deck."

Aunt Ivy shook her head. "I already know how to dance, and I've never liked water. Besides, I'm a free spirit. I don't like organized activities. I like to go where my inquisitive nature takes me."

Daisy sighed. She had a feeling her aunt's nature was going to send her investigating for the medallion.

But when everyone gathered for the treasure hunt, Daisy did not see Aunt Ivy. Otis gave each child a paper with the clues. The clues were in rhyme.

When you see rope, there is hope.
When water laps, and folks take naps
You're very near, and to the rear
Is food and drink, and a sink.

It's not too high, not in the sky.
It's below, but not too low.
That's the clue, good luck to you!

Otis reminded the children not to disturb anyone and that the treasure was not in any cabin or under anyone's deck chair. "When someone finds the treasure, we will blow the ship's whistle and announce the news over the loudspeaker."

Delphie had a new friend, named James, with him. He wore glasses and seemed to be very bright.

"I know where there's rope," James said.

He led the way to the rope, which was coiled up near the lifeboats on the side of the deck.

"Water laps here, too," James added.

"But there's no food around here," said Lois. "And no place for anyone to take a nap."

The children split up and looked everywhere. They looked under things and over things. They looked near the kitchens and into waste containers and on the shuffleboard court and even on the ship's stage.

Daisy looked around the pool because there was water and food and a rope on one of the rafts. But nothing that looked like a treasure was there. When she ran into Lois on the B Deck, Daisy said, "Maybe it's in the ship's basement."

Lois shook her head. "That's off-limits, that's what the guy said."

The girls met up with Delphie and James, and they decided to rest and have a drink. Some of the other treasure hunters joined them. One girl Daisy liked was called Rhonda. Aunt Ivy had told Daisy that Rhonda's parents were on the stage in New York City.

Then a boy whose name was Buzzy joined them. He seemed to have lots of ideas about where the treasure was hidden.

"I hear you won the lottery," he said to Lois.

"Not me," said Lois. "Her." Lois pointed to Daisy.

"My parents won," said Daisy, "but it was Lois's idea."

"That's cool," said Buzzy and asked Lois the details.

When Daisy and Lois got up to look for the treasure, Buzzy, Rhonda, James, and Delphie joined them.

As they walked along, Lois took Daisy aside and whispered, "Isn't he cute? Isn't Buzzy cute?"

What did Lois mean, cute? Buzzy looked like any other boy their age, Daisy thought. She didn't

consider ten-year-old boys "cute." Babies were cute and puppies were cute. Even Delphie could be cute at times. But Buzzy was, well, a little homely. His hair seemed to want to grow in different directions, and his ears stuck out.

Lois jabbed Daisy in the ribs with her elbow. "You know what I mean, *cute*, like for a boyfriend! I think he likes me."

Daisy couldn't believe her ears. Her mother had told her ten was way too young to think of having "boyfriends." It was all right to have friends who were boys, but not *boyfriends*, as Lois meant it. Both Daisy and Lois knew girls in their class who were boy crazy, but they were not friends of theirs. Now apparently *Lois* was turning into a boy-crazy girl!

"That's silly!" said Daisy. "You can't have a boyfriend yet."

"We're getting to that age when girls notice boys—we aren't kids anymore, you know," said Lois. "Jeannine Bonner wears lipstick, and she's eleven."

"Well I think it's dumb," said Daisy. "Anyway, he isn't even cute; his ears stick out. *And* he has braces on his teeth."

Lois stopped and stamped her foot. "Not cute

that way," she said. "Cute like, you know! Maybe I'll write to him if he gives me his address."

Daisy had had enough of this cute talk and decided to go up on the next deck by herself and look for the treasure behind the buffet table. No one would miss her. Lois was busy looking at Buzzy, and the others were talking about going to the gym to look, and then they could lift weights at the same time. Daisy did not want to lift weights.

When she got to the next deck, she had an idea. The long, white tablecloths on the buffet tables came to the floor. Underneath would be a perfect place to hide a treasure.

Daisy got down on her hands and knees and crawled under the table. It was dark and cozy, and she could hear voices in conversation above her. She remembered how Larkspur liked to sit at their feet under the table in the dining room, and she missed him. She wondered what he was doing and if Artie, Gladys, and Roxanne were feeding him things he liked.

All of a sudden, Daisy felt like she was not alone in this dark place. Someone was under this very table with her!

"*Pssst!*" said a voice. "Over here!"

It was too dark to see anyone. Daisy turned around, and bump! Her head hit someone else's head!

"Ouch!" cried a familiar voice.

"Aunt Ivy?" cried Daisy. "What are you doing under here?"

Daisy sat down and rubbed her head. Evidently Aunt Ivy was doing the same thing.

"I'm just—ah—taking notes for my class," said Aunt Ivy.

Daisy knew that Aunt Ivy was not under a buffet table doing homework in the dark.

"You are looking for the treasure!" accused Daisy. "That's illegal! Otis told you so!"

"Pooh," said Aunt Ivy. "It's a free country. Only allowing children to play is discrimination against adults. Did you know that?"

Daisy had counted on her mom to find an adult party for Aunt Ivy. Hadn't she done it? Daisy was all ready to chastise her aunt when, all of a sudden, the ship's whistle blew.

"Someone found the treasure!" said Daisy, crawling out from under the table. Aunt Ivy followed.

"Darn!" said Aunt Ivy. "I felt like I was on the right track!"

Static was coming from the intercom. Then a man's voice announced, "Will all of the children please come to the Hot Spot. I repeat, all children return to the Hot Spot. The treasure has been found. It has been found by . . ."

Here the man paused and whispered, "What were your names again?"

"The treasure has been found," he went on, "by Delton Green and James Hollaway."

CHAPTER 9

"Delton Green?" cried Daisy. "There's no Delton Green on the boat! I'll bet that's Delphie!"

Daisy ran as fast as she could to the Hot Spot, with Aunt Ivy at her heels.

Everyone was there, and, sure enough, there were Delphie and James up on the stage with the spotlight on them. Delphie was explaining his name to the announcer. "It's Delphie," he said, "not Delton."

Men with cameras were taking pictures of them for the *Cruise News*, the ship's newspaper that kept passengers up-to-date on what was happening aboard.

A reporter was interviewing the boys, and Delphie was explaining again about his name and that James was the one who thought of the ship's theater.

"There is a rope across the lobby," said James,

"and food and drinks at the popcorn counter. Water is lapping in the little fountain, and there's a sink in the rest room."

"Who is this Delton?" shouted Aunt Ivy, "and where do people take naps?"

"In the theater seats," said Delphie. "When the movie is boring. Aunt Ivy, what are you doing in the Hot Spot? This place is for kids!"

Aunt Ivy didn't seem to hear her nephew. Daisy was busy explaining the man's mistake with Delphie's name.

Everyone laughed about the boring-movie part, but they had to admit the boys were good detectives.

"We just looked behind the curtain on the stage, and there was the treasure!" said James. He held up the gold medallion. It sparkled in the sunlight.

"These boys will both get a gold medallion to remember this moment," said Otis. "They will also split the prize, which is a Toys for All Ages gift certificate for one hundred dollars—they each will get fifty—to use in the shop aboard the ship."

Everyone, especially Delphie and James, cheered.

"I'm going to get one of those creatures that turns into a truck!" shouted Delphie.

"I'm going to get that chess game with the marble bishops!" said James.

"I knew it was in the theater!" said Aunt Ivy. "That's where I was going to look next!"

Daisy was very glad her aunt didn't have the chance. It would be very embarrassing to have her onstage, getting a gift certificate for a toy shop or, worse yet, being disqualified and sent away, shouting about adult discrimination all over the boat!

When all the excitement was over, the children went back to their cabins and talked about the masquerade party. Lois talked about Buzzy. "I hope he is there," she said.

"You won't recognize him in a costume," said Daisy. "Unless his braces show."

As the children talked, the captain's voice came on the loudspeaker. "We have arrived at the island of Veneta," it said. "You are all free to go ashore for three hours. Buses will take you to the center of the island, where you can shop or take a sightseeing tour. Set your watches and be sure to be back on the buses in exactly three hours. We would not like to leave anyone on the island of Veneta."

The boat's whistle sounded with three loud toots. Aunt Ivy came dashing in from having a massage and said, "I'm going ashore! I hear Veneta has interesting volcanic formations."

"I don't care about Vulcans," said Delphie. "Dad said you can't go fishing, after all. The brochure lied. I'm going to the toy shop."

Daisy and Lois went with the Greens to see the volcanic remains but came back before the time was up.

"Nothing's as good as the ship," said Daisy.

"The ship with Buzzy on it!" giggled Lois.

Daisy was getting disgusted with Lois. She was no older than Daisy. Should Daisy be looking at cute boys, too? Was Lois ahead of her even in this? Daisy did not think boys were cute. Should she be interested in them, anyway? Would Lois find a handsome husband, and she, Daisy, be left behind?

Daisy sighed. Keeping up with Lois was a full-time job.

"I think we have to tell each other what kind of costume we are wearing for the party," said Lois. "I mean, first we're going trick-or-treating in our costumes, and we want to go together, don't we?"

Well, at least Lois still remembered her! She

wasn't thinking of going trick-or-treating with Buzzy instead of her best friend.

"OK," said Daisy. "Let's get out our costumes while Aunt Ivy is gone!"

The girls ran to get their boxes out of hiding. They took the costumes out and tried them on.

"Wow!" said Lois when they were ready. "A pirate! That's a great costume! Nobody will know it's you!"

Daisy wore big baggy pants, a black patch over one eye, and a sword in her belt. She had her hair pulled back under a turban.

There was no mistaking what Lois was. She had on a little frilly tutu, pink ballet shoes, a pink face mask, and her hair piled up on her head. She was a ballerina for the party. And a sort-of ballerina in real life. She used to take lessons every Tuesday in Liberty.

Suddenly there was a knock on the door.

"Hide!" said Lois.

"It's just me," called Aunt Ivy.

The girls got out of their costumes quickly and back into their regular clothes. Then Daisy opened the door.

"Your hair is all frowsy," said Aunt Ivy. "What have you girls been doing?"

"Just—not much," said Daisy.

"I thought maybe you'd show me your masquerade costumes," she whispered confidentially.

"We can't," said Lois. "It wouldn't be a masquerade if people knew it was us."

Aunt Ivy looked like she was pouting. She loved to be involved in the children's activities.

"I'm sorry," said Daisy. "But you can see us tomorrow, after the party."

Aunt Ivy sniffed. "I can't wait that long," she said, leaving the room.

Daisy stamped her foot. "She's so impatient!" she said.

"What does she mean, she can't wait that long?" said Lois, frowning.

"She probably just means she's excited to see how we're dressed," said Daisy.

"I wonder," said Lois. "It sounds fishy to me."

CHAPTER 10

But the next day the girls forgot Aunt Ivy's words; they were too busy thinking about the party.

The Hot Spot was decorated from top to bottom: colored lights were flashing, pumpkins were glaring, and ghosts were flapping in the air. Tables were set up to hold the Halloween food and drinks, barrels were brought in to bob for apples, and other games were set up. One game looked like *Wheel of Fortune*.

But before the party started, there was the fun of trick-or-treating on the ship.

"Just think," said Delphie. "Instead of walking down a street with houses, we're walking down a big hallway and going to cabins that are right on the ocean! If it rains or snows, it doesn't matter. We won't even have to cover up our costumes with jackets and raincoats like we did in Liberty."

"We won't run into any snow here on these sandy shores," laughed Aunt Ivy.

"What does she mean, 'we'?" whispered Lois. "Why didn't she say 'you'? We're the ones who are having a party!"

"It's just a figure of speech," said Daisy, quoting the line her aunt often used when Daisy didn't understand something she said.

"While you get dressed, we'll go out on the deck," said Mrs. Green. "So we don't see you. Unless, of course, you need help getting ready."

Delphie shook his head. "I'm going over to James's cabin," he said. "We're going together."

"We'll be fine," said Daisy.

"We are going to a Halloween movie in the theater," said Mr. Green. "A very scary one. We'll see you after the party. Otis promised there would be a parade on the Commodore Deck so the parents can see the costumes. Maybe one of you will win the prize for the best costume!"

Finally, everyone cleared out of the cabin. Aunt Ivy didn't say where she was going, but she left with the Greens.

The girls hurried into their costumes. Daisy helped Lois tie her ballet slippers and get her hair to stay on top of her head. Lois helped Daisy paint some make-believe blood on her sword.

They opened the cabin door and looked up and down the hallway. No one was in sight. They started out and took the glass elevator to the cabins where people were waiting for the goblins, ghosts, and other masqueraders to come to their doors. They were joined by a cat with a long bushy tail and someone dressed as a nuclear scientist. The girls knew he was a nuclear scientist because the sign on his white lab coat said so.

Coming down the hall was Humpty-Dumpty and a red eggplant.

As Daisy and Lois knocked on the first cabin door, the others joined them.

When the door opened, the children all shouted, "Tricks or treats! Money or eats!"

"Why look here, George," said a woman with pearls on. "We have a little pussycat, Humpty-Dumpty, a ballerina, and a pirate! And here comes a red apple!"

"Eggplant," said a familiar voice.

"I think the eggplant is Rhonda," whispered Lois.

Daisy was pretty sure Humpty-Dumpty was Buzzy, because she could see a wisp of hair that went the wrong way sticking out of his costume.

"That's Buzzy," whispered Daisy to Lois.

"Where?" she whispered back.

"Humpty-Dumpty," said Daisy.

Lois looked shocked. "He wouldn't be a nursery-rhyme character!" she said. "He'd be a knight or a rock star or something. That's definitely not Buzzy."

The man named George put a big candy bar in each Halloween bag and closed the door.

The group went on to the next door.

Two women opened the door. Before the children could say "trick or treat," one of the women said, "Come right in."

"Are we supposed to go in?" Daisy asked Lois.

"Well, they aren't exactly strangers," said Lois. "As your aunt said, we are all a big happy family on this cruise."

The children went in, and the woman shut the door as if they were guests who had come for the evening. It made Daisy uneasy. But there was nothing to be afraid of. It must be her imagination again, she thought.

"Sit down and make yourselves comfortable," said the woman. "My name is Marla, and this is my sister Rita."

The children nodded and shook hands with

both women. The cat was having trouble sitting down because its tail was in the way. Real cats had tails that fit around them neatly when they sat, but this cat didn't. Daisy was almost positive the cat was Delphie.

"Now!" said Rita. "Have a cookie and a glass of milk." She went from one child to the next with the tray. It even had a pot of tea on it for the two sisters.

"Marla is going to play a little selection for you on the piano, and then we will ask you to take your turn performing something for us! You have to earn your little treat!"

Now Daisy really was uneasy. It was not her imagination—these women had trapped them! What did they have to perform? Daisy could not play the piano! No one else made them earn their treats!

Daisy was cross. By leaps and bounds she was losing interest in this early Halloween. She was not going to any cabin except her own.

When they left, Daisy told Lois she didn't like earning her treats. "It was no big deal," said Lois.

"It was, too, a big deal," said Daisy crossly. "I'm not going to any more cabins."

She sat on a deck chair and waited for the

others. They came back loaded down with treats, and that made her feel worse.

"No one else made us come in," said Lois. "And a lot of them gave us dollar bills!"

This was definitely not the best Halloween Daisy had ever had. She hoped the party was going to be more fun than things were so far. Maybe she would have a good time and win some prizes. At least one.

CHAPTER 11

It was time for the party to begin. All of the children on the boat were heading toward the Hot Spot. There were prizefighters and boxers and tigers and green beans. There were doctors and dentists and Christmas trees and jack-o'-lanterns.

"Boy, I'm starving!" said the cat who was really Delphie.

"So am I!" said the nuclear scientist.

The two of them dashed right for the food table. It was loaded with pepperoni pizza, hot dogs, cheeseburgers, and french fries. Everyone dug in and loaded food onto orange pumpkin-shaped paper plates.

After they finished eating, there was a scary movie. And after that, there was more entertainment. A weight lifter lifted very heavy metal bars over his head. Then a juggler juggled balls and plates and even crystal wineglasses. A gymnast did pole vaults, somersaults, and handstands.

Everyone cheered and whistled and clapped after each act.

Then a clown came onstage and told jokes. He had a dog act with him.

"Larkspur could do those tricks if we taught him," Daisy whispered to Delphie.

"I'm not Delphie," said the cat, changing his voice. "I don't know who Larkspur is."

He didn't fool Daisy. She *could* be wrong, but she doubted it.

After the dog act, Otis announced they would bob for apples and play some other games. "We've got some great prizes," he said, "so don't be afraid to join in."

Lois and Daisy bobbed for apples, but all they got was wet.

"Those things are hard to get hold of," said Lois. "They sink every time you get near one."

The winner was the eggplant, and she got a fancy backpack to use for camping or for carrying books to school.

"I never win anything," said Daisy.

"Winning isn't everything," said Lois.

"Anyway, you won the lottery! That's about the best thing of all to win!"

But Daisy wanted to win something all on her own. Something that took more talent than just buying a ticket.

"Let's try to get those rings on the monkey's tail," said Daisy, trying to cheer up.

The girls got in line behind someone who was dressed like Sherlock Holmes, the detective. He had on a tweed coat and a plaid hat with earflaps that were tied on top of his head. In Holmes's mouth was a pipe. He had whiskers on his face, but Daisy wasn't sure they were real.

"I wonder who that is," said Daisy.

"I think it's Buzzy," said Lois. "That is something he would be. A detective. That's a real snazzy costume."

"Buzzy isn't Sherlock, he's Humpty-Dumpty, I'll bet you anything," said Daisy.

Lois stamped her foot. "He is *not!*" she said.

The detective's turn came, and he missed the monkey's tail with every one of his rings.

"Darn!" said Holmes.

Where had Daisy heard that voice before?

She didn't have time to think about it because it was her turn to throw the rings. She threw six and got only one on the tail. She got a small plastic boat that said Island Maiden on it.

"If you get all the rings on, you get a videotape of The Wizard of Oz with Judy Garland," said Lois. "I'm going to try to win that. I have this feeling I will."

Lois closed her eyes and concentrated. "I can see my rings on his tail," she chanted.

Then she picked up the rings and took her time. First she closed one eye. Then she stepped closer to the target. Then she stepped back. When she finally threw the rings, every one of them landed on the monkey's tail!

"You won it!" shouted Daisy. "You won The Wizard of Oz."

"I'll share it with you," said Lois kindly. "It's not your fault you're not psychic like me. We'll watch it together."

That would be fun, thought Daisy, but not as much fun as winning it herself.

"Look!" said Lois, pointing. "Buzzy is getting some pizza. I think I'll go over to him and tell him who I am."

Before Daisy could stop her, Lois ran over to the pizza table and sidled up to Sherlock.

"I know you're Buzzy," she said. "Remember

me from the treasure hunt? I'm Lois."

Sherlock didn't say anything. He just took more pizza.

"I know it's you," Lois teased. "You can't fool me."

Just then Humpty-Dumpty walked up to the table. He took a piece of pizza, and then he tapped Lois on the arm and said, "Hi, remember me?"

He gave Lois a big smile, and when he opened his mouth to do that, Daisy and Lois could both see, very clearly, a shining set of braces on his teeth! The only one on the ship with those braces was Buzzy!

CHAPTER 12

Lois looked shocked. She put her hand over her mouth and said, "Oh no! You can't be Buzzy!"

"I am," laughed Humpty-Dumpty, taking off his mask.

"Well, then, who is Sherlock Holmes?" asked Lois when she had got over the shock of liking a boy who would dress up as an egg.

"I don't know, but I have an idea," said Daisy.

Daisy began to follow Sherlock around.

"We're detectives following a detective," laughed Lois. "Aunt Ivy should be here; she loves spying on people. She could get points for her class!"

But soon the party was over, and it was time to go up on the deck for the parents' parade. As they lined up, Lois squeezed in next to Rhonda, but Daisy ran to catch up with Sherlock. Standing right beside him, she studied him carefully. She wished she could take off her turban; she was so warm. She noticed that Sherlock was opening his coat. It looked like real wool. Maybe it was the *real* Sherlock Holmes, thought Daisy!

It was her imagination again. Just because it was a good costume did not mean it was real. In fact, Holmes was a *fictional* detective! He never was real!

As Sherlock's coat swung open, Daisy noticed he had another kind of uniform on underneath. It looked familiar—and what was that pinned onto the collar?

It was a meter maid's pin! In fact, it was a meter maid's uniform! There was only one person on this boat, in fact, for miles around, who wore a meter maid's uniform and a meter maid's pin.

"Aunt Ivy!" she cried.

Before she could say more, someone pushed between them, and when Daisy turned around, Sherlock was gone!

She ran to find Lois and tell her the news.

"No way!" Lois replied. "It can't be, that's a guy!"

Daisy shook her head. "It's Aunt Ivy! She crashed our party!"

Now they were on deck, and the parents crowded around to see the costumes. Daisy and Lois could not find Aunt Ivy anywhere in the crowd. They saw Mr. and Mrs. Green, but Aunt Ivy was not with them. Daisy wondered why her parents did not wave to them, and then she remembered they didn't recognize them in costume!

"Now we will announce the winners of the prize for the best costumes!" called a man over the loudspeaker.

The first prize went to someone they did not know. She was dressed as a TV dinner.

"That is real originality!" laughed the host.

"The second prize goes to the pirate with blood on his sword!" he called.

"That's *you*!" shouted Lois, pushing her toward the stage.

It *was* Daisy! She had won something, after all! The crowd cheered as she went up to collect her prize. It was a good prize. It was a sweatshirt with a picture of the *Island Maiden* on the front of it.

When Daisy returned from the stage, the host was announcing the third, and last, prize.

"I'm looking for Sherlock Holmes," he said. "Has anyone seen him? He is wearing a quite authentic costume, complete with the pipe."

But Sherlock was nowhere to be found. Everyone remembered seeing him, but now he had disappeared.

And when Daisy found her parents again in the crowd, Aunt Ivy was with them! She had on her jeans and sailor shirt and sailor hat!

Daisy gave a sigh of relief. She could pretend she had imagined it all. Sherlock never existed. And just in time, before Aunt Ivy won an illegal prize!

But Daisy couldn't help wondering if her parents knew about Aunt Ivy's crashing the party. She was pretty sure they didn't. After all, it wasn't up to them to take care of her! They shouldn't have to watch Aunt Ivy like a child! She was an adult!

The host chose someone else for third place, and everyone pulled off their masks. Sure enough, Delphie was the cat, James was the scientist, Rhonda was the eggplant, and, of course, Buzzy was Humpty-Dumpty.

"Darn," said Lois. "And I thought he was so cute."

"He still looks the same," said Daisy. "He doesn't look any different just because he's not Sherlock."

"Yes he does," said Lois. "It's not cool to be an egg."

Lois was fickle, thought Daisy. If you really liked someone, a little thing like a costume shouldn't matter. But it would be a relief to have the old Lois back, the one who was not boy crazy.

All of the families started back to the cabins. The moon was hanging low over the ship, and the stars were twinkling. The water lapped the ship but didn't make anyone seasick. It was so beautiful that Daisy didn't want the trip to end. It would be a long time before she'd go to such a big Halloween party again.

But the cruise was soon coming to an end, like it or not, and Daisy tried to hold on to all the best memories. She tried to make her mind into a video camera and record the fun they'd had.

Back at the cabin, Daisy wanted to quiz Aunt Ivy about Sherlock Holmes, but she knew her aunt would deny it. And maybe she was right, maybe Daisy did imagine it was her. But she didn't think so. Anyway, she'd let sleeping dogs lie.

The next day Sally came around to collect the costumes and told them there was one more island stop before they headed back to Miami, which was what she considered home.

"If you don't want to tour the island," she said, "Otis is giving a little tour of the boat to those who remain. We don't want you saying good-bye to the *Island Maiden* without seeing all of her. You'll get a chance to see some of the little-known hideaway parts of the ship, where most of you haven't been. You know, like the sick bay and the captain's own quarters and down in the bowels of the ship, where the real machinery runs her."

"Who is 'her'?" asked Delphie.

"Ships are called 'her,'" said Sally, "and 'she.' It's the custom."

"Sometimes my dad calls our car 'she,'" said Lois. "Like *she* needs new tires soon."

"Well, we're all going to the island," said Mr. Green. "That is, your mom and Aunt Ivy and me. You children can do whatever you like. Time is going fast now; we have to squeeze last-minute fun in before it's over."

"I want to go in the bowels," said Delphie. "Maybe the guy down there will let me steer the ship."

Mr. Green laughed. "Don't steer us into an iceberg," he said.

CHAPTER 13

"There are no icebergs! Are there, Dad?" asked Delphie.

"No, I don't think so," said Mr. Green.

"Not around here," laughed Sally. "And no one steers the boat anymore; it's all automatic, like a plane."

Daisy had seen the sick bay. That's where Aunt Ivy went when they first came aboard. But there were a lot of nooks and crannies she had not seen.

"Let's go on the tour," said Daisy to Lois.

"I don't know . . . ," she said.

"Maybe Buzzy will be there," said Daisy.

Daisy waited for Lois to say she didn't care about Buzzy anymore.

But she didn't.

Instead she said, "I guess we could go. Maybe I could give Buzzy another chance."

When they got to the Hot Spot, Buzzy was there, along with James, Rhonda, and some others. He seemed glad to see them.

Lois took one look him and rolled her eyes.

"He is a baby!" she said to Daisy. "I can't get over that he was Humpty Dumpty."

When everyone had arrived, Otis and some of the other nannies counted noses to be sure they ended up with the same number of children they had started with. Then the tour set off for the ship's medical office. There the doctor on board told them how they were equipped for emergencies.

"We can even do minor surgery right aboard the ship," he boasted. "We have our own backup generator in case power goes out, and of course we have a dentist in case of dental emergencies."

"What if someone has a baby on board?" asked Lois.

The doctor frowned. "Well, we could take care of that, but we hope it won't happen," he said.

One of the smaller children said, "You can't get babies on a boat; you get them in a hospital. That's where my mom got our baby."

A boy called Teddy said that was wrong, that Big Bird brought their baby, and the two began to argue.

Otis had to step in and tell them they were both right.

"People get babies in different places," he said.

"I know," said a girl named Natalie. "We got our baby in Korea."

The doctor looked glad to see the tour move on to the barbershop. The barber gave them each some candy and said to come back and get a haircut if they needed one.

The next stop was the captain's quarters, where they saw maps on the wall with small pins in them to show where they had been and where they were going. There was a computer running and a fax machine clicking away. Phones were ringing, and stewards with questions were knocking on the door.

"The captain is like the hub of the boat," said Otis. "He has to see that everyone works together to make things run smoothly."

In the big galley of the ship, the tour watched the chefs prepare dinner. Some of the cooks were even at work cutting up fresh vegetables for the following day. There were hot rolls baking and turkey roasting and a tall roast beef being carved. Another cook was making radishes into little roses, and another was squeezing cheese out of a

little tube onto crackers. He gave one to everyone.

When they had finished there, Otis led the tour onto the glass elevator. He pressed a button, and the elevator seemed to be dropping into the depths of the ship.

When the doors opened, Daisy and Lois and Delphie all recognized the long dark passage that looked like a tunnel from when they mistakenly came down here the last time.

"There's that guy in overalls who told us we couldn't be down here," said Daisy.

Sure enough, the man who had told them this area was off-limits was back. But he didn't look so mean this time. A tag on his shirt said his name was Paul, and he was smiling.

As Otis led the group on, they saw lots of big machines. These were the machines that ran the ship.

Paul talked about how the ship ran and how much fuel it took.

"It takes a lot of fuel to move sixty thousand tons!" he said. "We usually cruise at twenty-four knots. It's like moving a small city through the water!"

Delphie gave a long, low whistle of amazement.

Paul let the children pull some handles and

turn some wheels. He showed them a whole wall of gauges, buttons, and levers. He showed them how to read which direction they were traveling in and the force of the wind.

When they were through, they got back on the elevator and went to the main deck.

"Well, I'm glad we found out why it was off-limits," said Daisy. Daisy liked things to end well. She hated what Aunt Ivy called "loose ends."

As everyone was starting back to their own cabins, a woman came running through the crowd and grabbed Buzzy.

"It's time for a little nap," she said, hustling him toward their cabin.

"Aw, Mom," said Buzzy. Halfway down the hall, he turned around and called to Lois. "I'll see you later," he shouted.

"In your dreams," she muttered to Daisy. "He's a real mama's boy."

The next day was the last day aboard. Delphie spent the time in the gym, but the girls went swimming in the pool, played tennis in the Hot Spot, and just lay in deck chairs looking at the blue water and blue, blue sky. They exchanged names and addresses with the friends they'd met, so they could write to them.

Then the cruise-ship company took some last-minute pictures of them all having fun.

Before long, suitcases began to appear on deck and cabin boys carried them from the staterooms.

Daisy packed the last souvenir in her bag and went to help Aunt Ivy, who had lots of souvenirs that would not fit in her suitcase.

"Put some in your carry-on bag," suggested Lois. "Or in your purse."

"The purse you left home on the table," giggled Delphie.

As the girls helped her, Daisy spied something lumpy in one of Aunt Ivy's bags. She lifted up a pair of her shoes, and saw—a pipe! It was Sherlock Holmes's pipe! Daisy poked Lois and motioned with her eyes.

Lois looked shocked. "You were right!" she whispered. "Aunt Ivy was Sherlock! You didn't imagine it!"

Daisy decided not to mention the find to Aunt Ivy.

When the boat docked, a band was playing. Daisy felt like a seasoned sailor. The captain and his crew stood on the deck saying good-bye. They shook hands with all the passengers, just as they had when they'd boarded.

"So Poison Ivy is leaving us!" called Ralph, with a big grin. "Come back on a trip with us again!"

Aunt Ivy turned bright red. As the cameraman filmed the last shots, Delphie chanted, "Poison Ivy! Poison Ivy! Poison Ivy! That's a great name for our aunt!"

Mrs. Green shot Delphie a warning look. Then she said, "Here we are on dry land again!" as she walked down the gangplank onto the dock.

"It feels funny to walk on the ground!" said Delphie, staggering around.

"It's like we've got rubber legs!" said his mom.

"It's good to be home!" said Mr. Green, even though they were only in Miami. It would be a few more hours till they arrived in St. Paul.

The cruise was over, thought Daisy, and maybe her sweet family would settle down now and stay home, and life would return to normal. Of course, school was coming up, in a new city. And Lois always was looking for new ways to spend the lottery money.

She watched Lois saying good-bye to Rhonda, Buzzy, and Buzzy's mother. Then Lois ran and caught up with the Greens.

"Terra firma!" Lois shouted as her feet touched land.

With Lois around, things probably would never return to normal. Daisy knew that, given her friend's psychic ability, change was bound to happen. They could all end up in darkest Africa, or Buckingham Palace—or even the White House!

Only time would tell.